EARLY BIRD
STORIES

Bad Dog
&
No, Nell, No!

Early★Reader

First American edition published in 2019 by Lerner Publishing Group, Inc.

An original concept by Elizabeth Dale
Copyright © 2019 Elizabeth Dale

Illustrated by Julia Seal

First published by Maverick Arts Publishing Limited

Maverick
arts publishing

Licensed Edition
Bad Dog & No, Nell, No!

Lerner Publications Company
A division of Lerner Publishing Group, Inc.
241 First Avenue North
Minneapolis, MN 55401 USA

For reading levels and more information, look up this title at
www.lernerbooks.com.

Main body text set in Mikado a. Typeface provided by HVD Fonts.

Library of Congress Cataloging-in-Publication Data
Names: Dale, Elizabeth, 1952– author. | Seal, Julia, illustrator. | Dale, Elizabeth, 1952– Bad dog. | Dale, Elizabeth, 1952– No, Nell, no!
Title: Bad dog ; and No, Nell, no! / by Elizabeth Dale ; illustrated by Julia Seal.
Description: First American edition, licensed edition. | Minneapolis, MN : Lerner Publishing Group, Inc., 2019. | Series: Early bird readers. Yellow (Early bird stories).
Identifiers: LCCN 2018017788 (print) | LCCN 2018026029 (ebook) | ISBN 9781541543225 (eb pdf) | ISBN 9781541541610 (lb : alk. paper) | ISBN 9781541546196 (pb : alk. paper)
Subjects: LCSH: Readers—Animals. | Readers (Primary) | Animals—Juvenile literature.
Classification: LCC PE1127.A6 (ebook) | LCC PE1127.A6 D224 2019 (print) | DDC 428.6/2—dc23

LC record available at https://lccn.loc.gov/2018017788

Manufactured in the United States of America
1-45335-38985-5/29/2018

EARLY BIRD
STORIES

Bad Dog
&
No, Nell, No!

Elizabeth Dale

Illustrated by
Julia Seal

Lerner Publications ◆ Minneapolis

The Letter "D"

Trace the lowercase and uppercase letter with a finger. Sound out the letter.

Around,
up,
down

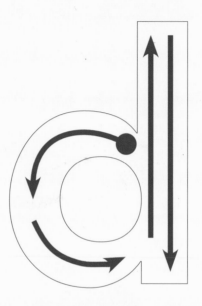

Down,
up,
around

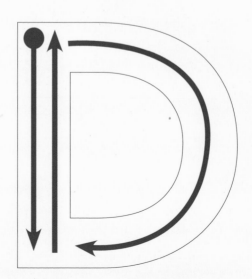

Some words to familiarize:

car flower chair

High-frequency words:

the   on   dad

Tips for Reading *Bad Dog*

- Practice the words listed above before reading the story.

- If the reader struggles with any of the other words, ask them to look for sounds they know in the word. Encourage them to sound out the words and help them read the words if necessary.

- After reading the story, ask the reader what the dog was doing.

Fun Activity

Discuss how everyone could teach the dog to be better behaved.

Bad Dog

The bad dog sits on the car.

The bad dog sits on the flowers.

The bad dog sits on Dad!

The Letter "N"

Trace the lowercase and uppercase letter with a finger. Sound out the letter.

Down,
up,
around,
down

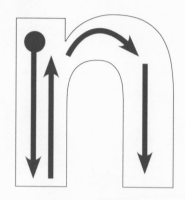

Down,
up,
down,
up

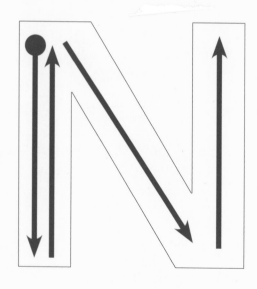

Some words to familiarize:

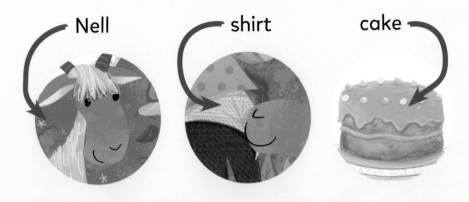

Nell   shirt   cake

High-frequency words:

no   this

Tips for Reading *No, Nell, No!*

- Practice the words listed above before reading the story.

- If the reader struggles with any of the other words, ask them to look for sounds they know in the word. Encourage them to sound out the words and help them read the words if necessary.

- After reading the story, ask the reader why Nell did not want to eat her dinner at the end.

Fun Activity

What are your favorite things to eat?

No, Nell, No!

Nell eats this bag.

Nell eats this sock.

Nell eats this shirt.

Nell eats this hat.

No, Nell, no!

Nell eats this cake.

Leveled for Guided Reading

Early Bird Stories have been edited and leveled by leading educational consultants to correspond with guided reading levels. The levels are assigned by taking into account the content, language style, layout, and phonics used in each book.

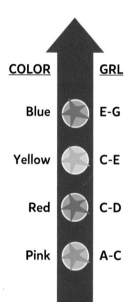

COLOR		GRL
Blue		E-G
Yellow		C-E
Red		C-D
Pink		A-C